This Walker book belongs to:

. . . .

. . . .

. . . .

For Kurt, who celebrates
B. B.

For Florey and Mickey
K. D.

First published 2012 by Walker Books Ltd
87 Vauxhall Walk, London SE11 5HJ

This edition published 2013

2 4 6 8 10 9 7 5 3 1

Text © 2009 Bonny Becker
Illustrations © 2009 Kady MacDonald Denton

The right of Bonny Becker and Kady MacDonald Denton to be identified
as author and illustrator respectively of this work has been asserted by them
in accordance with the Copyright, Designs and Patents Act

This book has been typeset in New Baskerville

Printed in China

British Library Cataloguing in Publication Data:
a catalogue record for this book is available from the British Library

ISBN 978-1-4063-4539-1

www.walker.co.uk

A Birthday for Bear

Bonny Becker

illustrated by

Kady MacDonald Denton

WALKER BOOKS
AND SUBSIDIARIES
LONDON • BOSTON • SYDNEY • AUCKLAND

S*wish! Swish! Swish!* Bear dusted his shelves. *Whisk! Whisk! Whisk!* Bear swept his floor. He was very, very busy today. Bear was always very, very busy on his birthday. He heard a *tap, tap, tapping* on his front door.

He opened the door and there was Mouse, small and grey and bright-eyed.

"Happy birthday, Bear!" cried Mouse.

"It's not my birthday," lied Bear.

"But it says so right here," said Mouse, waving a party invitation.

"Let me see that!" demanded Bear.

He peered at the card. It read:

> *Dear Mouse,*
> *Come to Bear's birthday at Bear's house today!*
> *Balloons and presents and birthday cake.*

"This is your handwriting!" protested Bear. "*You* wrote it."

"Did I?" asked Mouse, most innocently.

"Yes," said Bear. He sounded quite certain.

Mouse hung his head. "Shameful trickery," he confessed. "Terribly sorry. But perhaps we could have just a *little* birthday party?"

"I do not like parties. I do not like birthdays. And I especially do not like birthday parties for me at my house," Bear announced, and he swept Mouse out of the door.

Slop! Slop! Slop! Bear mopped the hallway. He heard a *tap, tap, tapping* on his back door.

He opened the door, and there stood a tiny delivery-man holding three red balloons.

"Happy Birthday balloons for a Mr Bear," announced the delivery-man.

Bear narrowed his eyes. "You are not a delivery-man. You are Mouse! I can see your tail," he declared, pointing an accusing claw.

Mouse hung his head. "Deepest apologies," he said. "But surely you would like just one balloon? It bats about quite nicely."

"I do not like balloons. I do not like parties. And I do not like birthdays,"
said Bear. He shut the back door with a firm bang.

Slosh! Slosh! Slosh! Bear scrubbed the counters and washed the dishes.

He heard a *rap, rap, rapping* on his kitchen window.

Bear opened his window. There stood a little postman holding a bright red envelope. "A Birthday Greeting for Bear," said the postman, reading the envelope.

Bear crossed his arms. "You are not
the postman. You are Mouse!" he cried.
"I can see your ears."

"Appalling behaviour—" Mouse started to say,
but Bear slammed the shutters.

Squidjedy! Squidjedy! Squidjedy! Bear polished his living-room clock.

What a very, very busy day he was having.

Bear pricked up his ears. There was a *scritch, scritch, scratching* sound coming from his fireplace.

On to the hearth bounced a tiny Santa Claus!

"Ho! Ho! Ho!" cried the little Santa Claus. "A Christmas present for Bear!"

Christmas already? thought Bear. He reached for the present, then snatched back his paw. "Wait a minute," he growled. "It's not Christmas. It's my birthday!"

"You said it *wasn't* your birthday!" The little Santa looked very pleased with himself.

Bear glared. "Well, you are not Santa," he shouted. "You are Mouse. I can see your whiskers!"

"Ah, you are too clever for me, Bear," Mouse admitted. "But still, you must like birthday presents. Everyone likes a present."

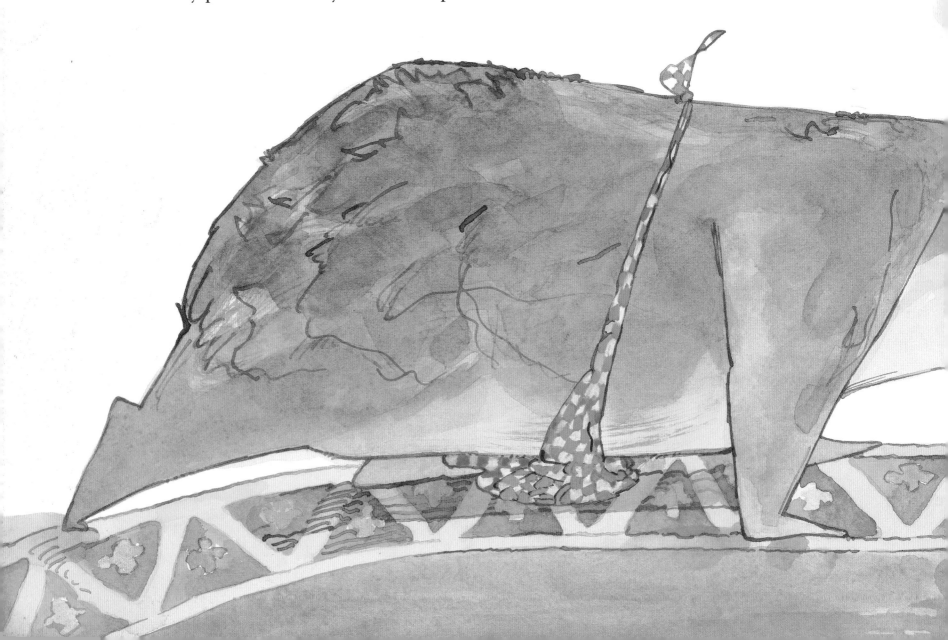

Bear pulled himself up to his full height and roared,

"I do not like presents.

I do not like birthday cards.

I do not like balloons.

I do not like parties.

I do not like BIRTHDAYS!"

"And look! You've scattered ashes all over my nice clean hearth!"

Bear trembled with anger. "I am very, very, VERY busy today!"

"It's quite a lovely present," Mouse said, and he sadly dragged it away.

Bear scowled and swept up the ashes from the hearth. No more mouse prints. Good!

Bear's paw slowed to a stop. No one had ever given Bear a present before.

Bear swallowed. He had noticed it was an especially big present, too.

He wondered what sort of especially big present it might be.

Ding-dong went the doorbell.

Bear opened the door. There on the step was a pink box.

"You don't fool me, Mouse! I know you're in there!" Bear cried, springing open the lid of the box.

But inside was just a cake. A big cake with chocolate sprinkles and the words "HAPPY BIRTHDAY, BEAR" in chocolate icing.

"I do not like birthday cake, either!" Bear announced loudly so Mouse could hear.

Bear glared into the bushes, looked
behind the door, peeked under the box.
No postmen, no delivery-men, no Santas.
No Mouse.

Bear picked up the box and hurried
to the kitchen.

Bear glanced around, then lifted out the cake. He scooped up a pawful of creamy icing and was just about to plop it into his mouth, when—

Out of the cake popped Mouse! Small and grey and bright-eyed!

"A-haa!" cried Mouse. "You *do* like birthday cake!"

Bear looked down at the chocolate cake with chocolate icing

and chocolate sprinkles.

"I made it myself," added Mouse with an eager flick of his tail.

No one had ever made Bear a birthday cake before.

Even so, Bear started to say, "I am very, very busy today" – but then

he didn't. "Chocolate is my favourite," he admitted.

Mouse flicked his tail and whisked out of the door.

Quick as a whisker, Mouse was back. He tied three red balloons
to Bear's chair, plonked a sparkly birthday hat on Bear's head
and set the especially big present on Bear's lap.
Bear lifted the lid from his present. *Crickle. Crackle. Crinkle.* He parted
the crisp white paper.

In the box nestled a pair of shiny red roller skates – just the right size for a bear.

"Happy birthday!" cried Mouse.

"Thank you, Mouse," said Bear gruffly. "I've always wanted a pair of shiny red

roller skates." Bear cleared his throat. "Perhaps I don't mind birthdays after all."

Then Bear cut a big slice of cake for himself and an especially big slice for Mouse.

And Bear and Mouse ate the whole cake – every sprinkle and crumb.